To Tim – J. C.

Text and illustrations copyright © Jane Chapman 2012
Original edition published in English by Little Tiger Press,
an imprint of Magi Publications, London, England, 2012
LTP/1500/0288/1011 • Printed in Singapore

Library of Congress Cataloging-in-Publication Data available.

Very Special Friends

Jane Chapman

Good Books

Intercourse, PA 17534, 800/762-7171
www.GoodBooks.com

One morning, Mouse hopped to the edge of the river. And there she sat, waiting for her Special Friends.

Dragonflies zipped over the rushes.
Tadpoles plipped in the shallows.
Water splashed softly against
the rocks.

"Hello," said Rabbit.
"What are you doing?"
  "I'm waiting for my Special
Friends," said Mouse.

"Then I will wait with you,"
said Rabbit. "May I?"

Butterflies fluttered on the breeze.
Bees buzzed in the daisies.
Ants scuttled busily in the grass.

"Oh, it's you!" laughed Frog.
"What are you doing?"

"We're waiting for Mouse's
Special Friends," said Rabbit.
"Just the weather for waiting,"
smiled Frog. "May I join you?"

Sunshine speckled the trees.
Caterpillars munched lazily in the leaves.
A single cloud drifted in the blue, blue sky.

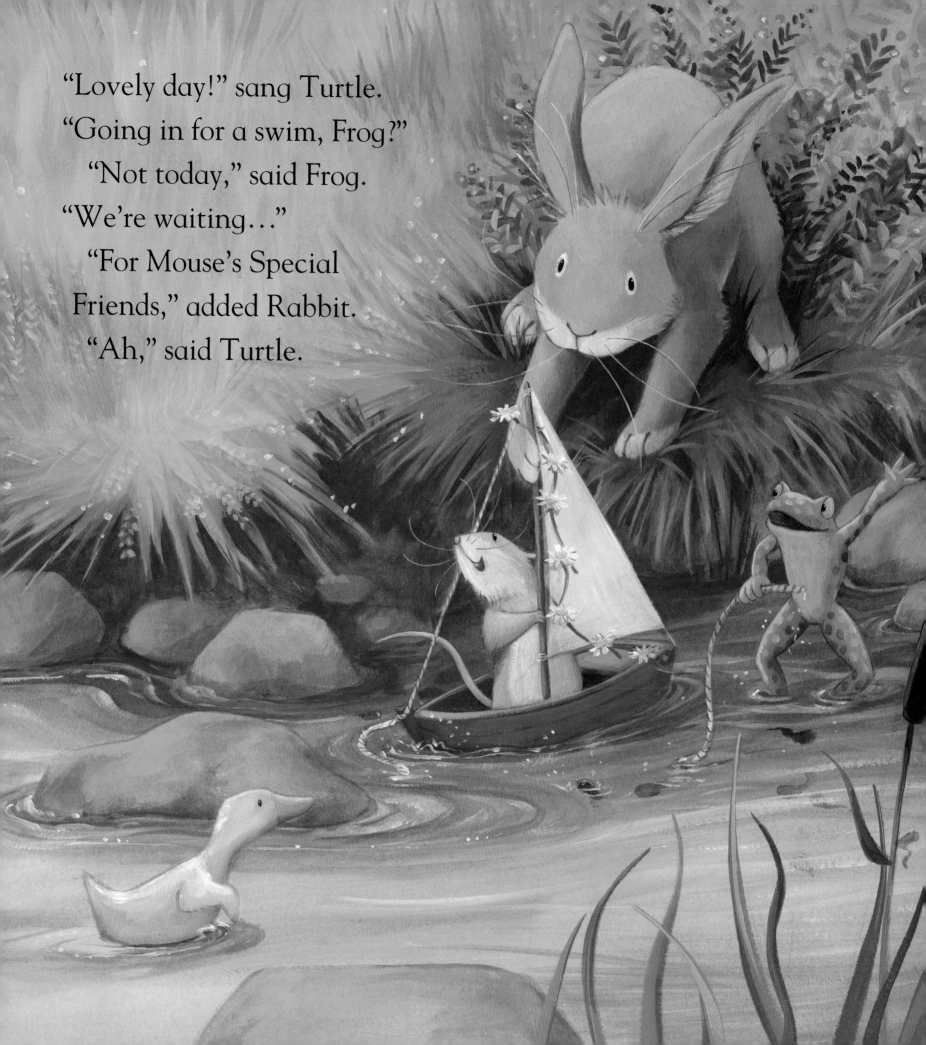

"Lovely day!" sang Turtle.
"Going in for a swim, Frog?"
   "Not today," said Frog.
"We're waiting…"
   "For Mouse's Special
Friends," added Rabbit.
   "Ah," said Turtle.

It was peaceful on the riverbank.
Turtle shared his lunch, and when
everyone was full, the ducklings
cleaned up the crumbs.

"Mmmmmm, delicious," sighed Rabbit.
"Perfect," whispered Frog.
"You picked a lovely spot for waiting,
Mouse," said Turtle.
"I did," said Mouse.

Shadows edged toward the water.
Fireflies glittered like stars.

The sun glowed warmly and sank
behind the trees.

Mouse stretched her arms out wide
and stood up.

"Well, I must be off," she said.

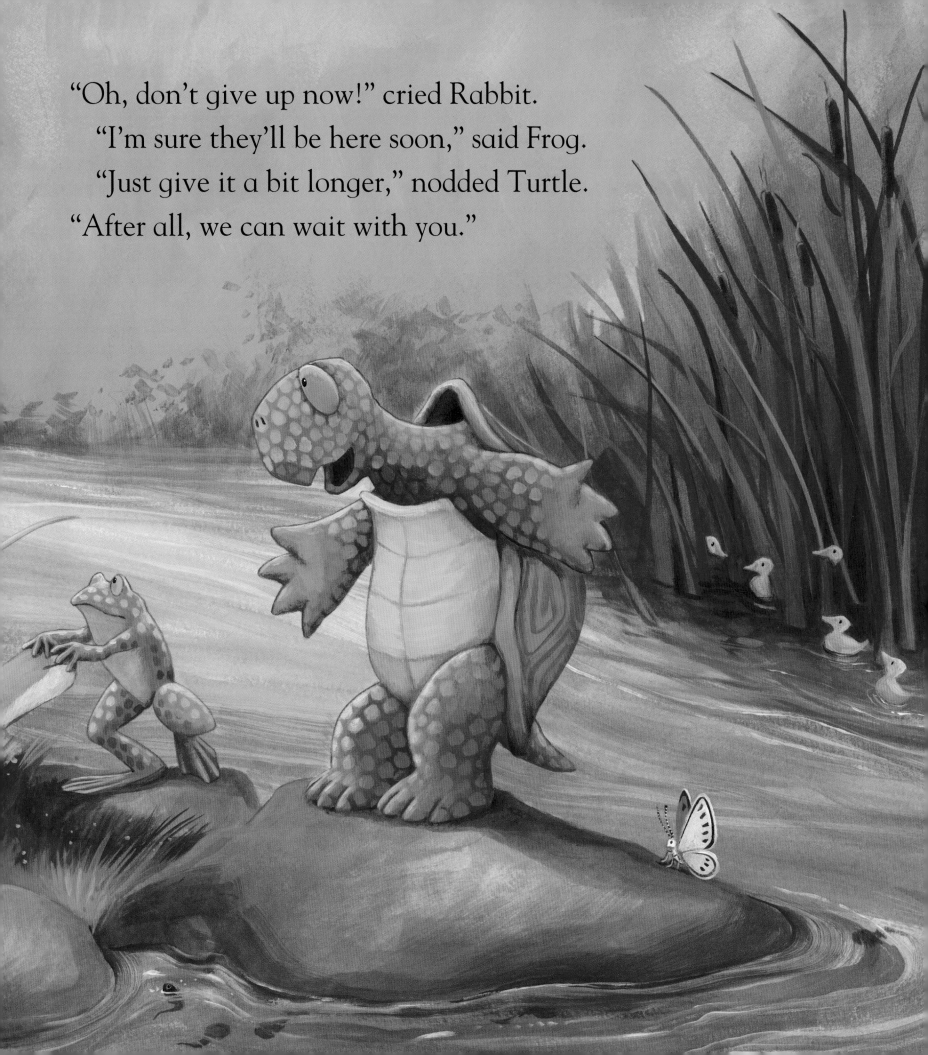

"Oh, don't give up now!" cried Rabbit.
"I'm sure they'll be here soon," said Frog.
"Just give it a bit longer," nodded Turtle.
"After all, we can wait with you."

"Wait for what?" asked Mouse.
"Your Special Friends, of
course!" said Rabbit.

"But you're all here!"
Mouse smiled.

"Rabbit…"

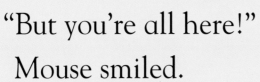

"and Frog…"

"and Turtle…"

"Who could be more
special than you?"
A rosy glow spread
over three faces.

"It has been a Special Day," said Rabbit.
"Let's wait again tomorrow!" laughed Frog.
"With apple cake," added Turtle.
"See you tomorrow then," said Mouse.
And with a happy wave she turned
towards home.

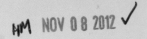